MARC BROWN

# D.W. Saves the Day

D.W. and Grandma Thora were going to the park for a picnic. "I have the food," said D.W.

"I told Mrs. Tibble and the twins to meet us at the park," said Grandma Thora.

"Oh, no!" thought D.W. "Not the Tibble Twins!"

Eliza

When D.W. got to the park, the Tibble Twins were nowhere in sight. Arthur was playing baseball.

"Hey, Arthur," called D.W. "Want a sandwich?"

"Strike three!" Francine shouted. "You're out!"

Arthur turned to look at his sister.

"Thanks a lot, D.W.!" yelled Arthur.

Then suddenly D.W. heard screaming and ducks squawking.

“Hi, D.W.!” screamed the Tibble Twins.

“Leave those poor ducks alone!” said D.W.

Soon the Tibble Twins got bored chasing ducks.

"Let's play florist," said Tommy. They began pulling flowers out of the ground and stomping on plants.

D.W. couldn't believe her eyes.

The Tibble Twins ran to the sandbox.

"Let's bury D.W.!" squealed Tommy.

"No," said Timmy. "Let's bury the grass!"

They started to shovel all the sand onto the grass.

"Stop!" D.W. cried. "The grass doesn't like that!"

“Time for lunch!” called Grandma Thora.

“Saved by a sandwich,” said D.W.

“I’m hungry!” cried Tommy.

“Me, too!” cried Timmy.

In seconds, food was everywhere.

CHIPS

CHIPS

But the Tibble Twins couldn't sit still for long.

"Let's catch butterflies!" they shouted.

"Those poor butterflies!" D.W. thought.

Then D.W. got an idea. “Do you guys want to hear a story?” she called.

“We love stories,” said Tommy.

"Once upon a time..." D.W. began in her sweetest voice. "There was a giant called Mother Nature."

"A *real* mother?" asked Tommy.

"Oh, yes," said D.W. "She was the mother of all the flowers and animals in the whole wide world."

“She watered her flowers with a giant watering can,” said D.W.

“Is that why it rains?” asked Timmy.

“Of course,” D.W. said. “Now stop interrupting me.”

GLUE

"So..." D.W. continued, "Mother Nature took all the little green caterpillars and glued wings on them."

"To make butterflies?" asked Tommy.

"Yes," D.W. said. "Then she touched all the teeny-tiny flower buds with her magic wand and turned them into big roses."

"Everything was beautiful and just right..." D.W. explained. "Until two very naughty boys began to mess with Mother Nature's things!"

The Tibble Twins gulped.

"They tore up her flowers, chased her little ducks, and threw trash everywhere! That made her really mad!"

"Uh-oh," said Tommy.

"Oops!" said Timmy.

"Then what happened?" asked the twins.

"She turned herself into a little spider," said D.W., "and grew and grew until she was as big as a...brontosaurus. Then she spun a giant web that trapped those little boys!"

"Look! A spider!" screamed Tommy. He pointed to a little spider crawling up D.W.'s arm.

"It's Mother Nature!" screamed Timmy.

"She's after us!" cried Tommy.

“Run for your life!” The Tibble Twins yelled.

D.W. smiled.

“Hi, Mother Nature,” said Arthur. He waved to the spider.

“We’re sorry, Mother Nature,” called the Tibble Twins. “We promise to be nice to all your stuff from now on!”

"Gee," said D.W. "I'm a better storyteller than I thought."

"You dropped something, Arthur," said D.W. "And I'd pick it up if I were you...because Mother Nature is always watching."